Jon Scieszka's TRUCKTOWN

KAT'S MYSTERY GIFT

WRITTEN BY JON SCIESZKA

CHARACTERS AND ENVIRONMENTS DEVELOPED BY THE

DAVID SHANNON   **LOREN LONG**   **DAVID GORDON**

ILLUSTRATION CREW:

Executive producer: Keytoon, Inc. in association with Animagic S.L.

Creative supervisor: Sergio Pablos ○ Drawings by: Juan Pablo Navas ○ Color by: Isabel Nadal

Color assistant: Gabriela Lazbal ○ Art director: Karin Paprocki

READY-TO-ROLL

ALADDIN

NEW YORK   LONDON   TORONTO   SYDNEY

ALADDIN

An imprint of Simon & Schuster

Children's Publishing Division

1230 Avenue of the Americas, New York, NY 10020

First Aladdin paperback edition October 2009

Text and illustrations copyright © 2009 by JRS Worldwide, LLC.

ALADDIN is a trademark of Simon & Schuster, Inc., and related logo is a registered trademark of Simon & Schuster, Inc.

READY-TO-READ is a registered trademark of Simon & Schuster, Inc.

TRUCKTOWN and JON SCIESZKA'S TRUCKTOWN and design are trademarks of JRS Worldwide, LLC.

For information about special discounts for bulk purchases, please contact Simon & Schuster Special Sales at 1-866-506-1949
or business@simonandschuster.com.

The Simon & Schuster Speakers Bureau can bring authors to your live event. For more information or to book an event
contact the Simon & Schuster Speakers Bureau at 1-866-248-3049 or visit our website at www.simonspeakers.com.

The text of this book was set in Truck King. / Manufactured in the United States of America / 10 9 8 7 6 5 4 3 2

Library of Congress Cataloging-in-Publication Data / Scieszka, Jon.

Kat's mystery gift / written by Jon Scieszka ; characters and environments developed by Design Garage: David Shannon,
Loren Long, David Gordon. – 1st Aladdin Paperbacks ed. / p. cm. – (Trucktown) (Ready-to-roll)

Summary: The trucks speculate about what could be inside a beautifully wrapped gift box.

[1. Gifts–Fiction. 2. Trucks–Fiction.] I. Design Garage. II. Title.

PZ7.S41267Kat 2009 / [E]–dc22 / 2007027801

ISBN 978-1-4169-4143-9 (pbk) / ISBN 978-1-4169-4154-5 (lib)

1109 LAK

Kat has a gift.

The gift is red.

And square.
And a mystery.

"What is inside?"
asks Gabby.

"That," says Kat,
"is the mystery."

"I guess it is a new horn,"
says Gabby.
"Could be," says Kat.

"I guess it is a new ball," says Rosie.

"Could be," says Kat.

"I guess it
is new tires,"
says Pete.

"Could be,"
says Kat.

"New sirens?" guesses Pat.
"New lights?" guesses Lucy.

"Could be . . . and could be," says Kat.

"But it could be a jewel,"
says Kat.

"Or a cloud…"

"A giant teddy bear?"

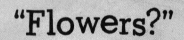

"Flowers?"

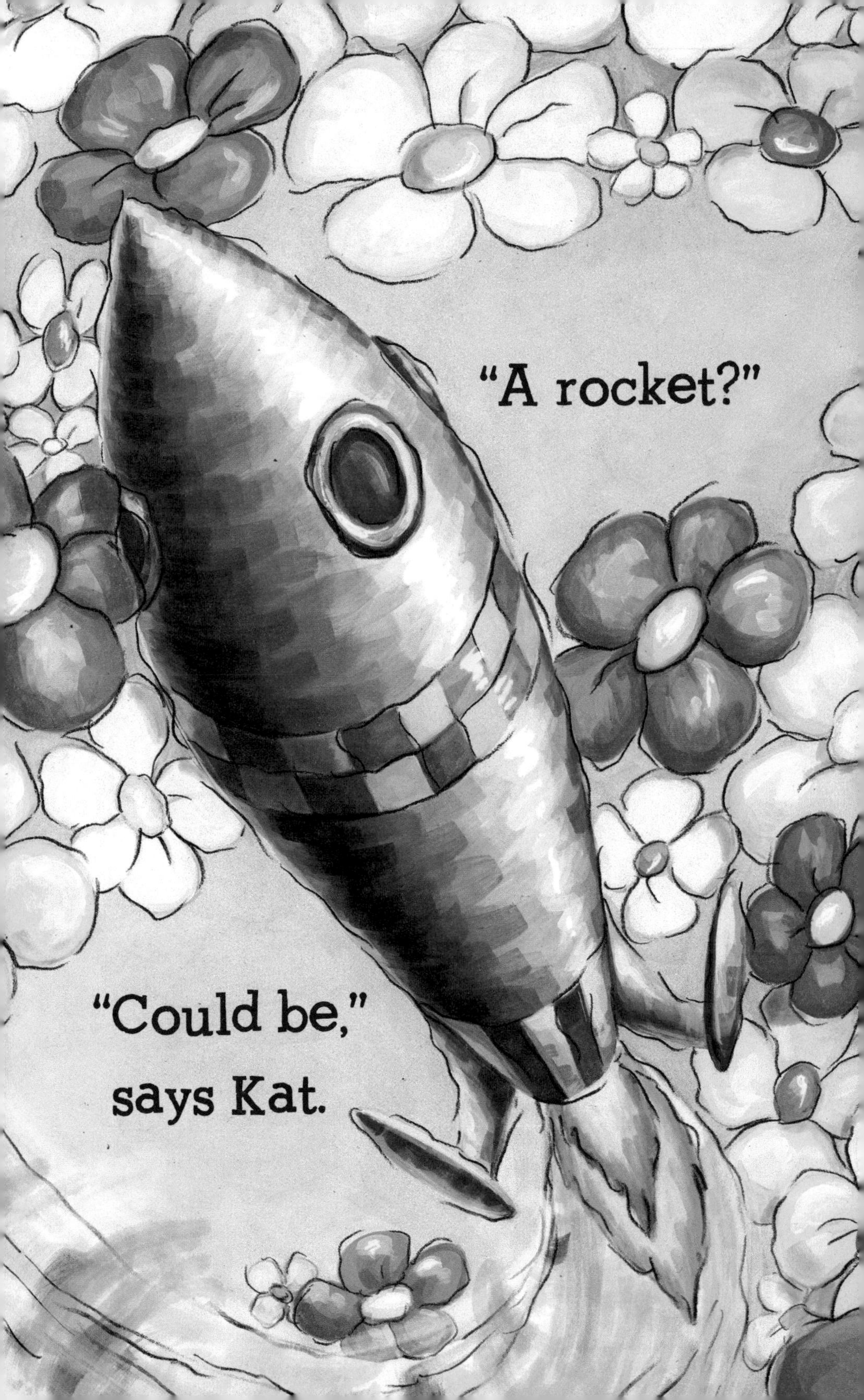

"A rocket?"

"Could be,"
says Kat.

"WOW!"

says Gabby.

"Open it, open it,
open it now!"
they all cheer.
"We could . . . ," says Kat.